A Note to Parents

Reading books aloud and playing word games are two valuable ways parents can help their children learn to read. The easy-to-read stories in the **My First Hello Reader! With Flash Cards** series are designed to be enjoyed together. Six activity pages and 16 flash cards in each book help reinforce phonics, sight vocabulary, reading comprehension, and facility with language. Here are some ideas to develop your youngster's reading skills:

Reading With Your Child

- Read the story aloud to your child and look at the colorful illustrations together. Talk about the characters, setting, action, and descriptions. Help your child link the story to events in his or her own life.
- Read parts of the story and invite your child to fill in the missing parts. At first, pause to let your child "read" important last words in a line. Gradually, let your child supply more and more words or phrases. Then take turns reading every other line until your child can read the book independently.

Enjoying the Activity Pages

- Treat each activity as a game to be played for fun. Allow plenty of time to play.
- Read the introductory information aloud and make sure your child understands the directions.

Using the Flash Cards

- Read the words aloud with your child. Talk about the letters and sounds and meanings.
- Match the words on the flash cards with the words in the story.
- Help your child find words that begin with the same letter and sound, words that rhyme, and words with the same ending sound.
- Challenge your child to put flash cards together to make sentences from the story and create new sentences.

Above all else, make reading time together a fun time. Show your child that reading is a pleasant and meaningful activity. Be generous with your praise and know that, as your child's first and most important teacher, you are contributing immensely to his or her command of the printed word.

—Tina Thoburn, Ed.D.
Educational Consultant

Library of Congress Cataloging-in-Publication Data

Packard, David.
The ball game / by David Packard / illustrated by R. W. Alley.
p. cm.
Summary: A young player steps up to bat at a crucial point in a baseball game and succeeds in making the play that wins the game.
ISBN 0-590-46190-7
[1. Baseball—Fiction. 2. Stories in rhyme.] I. Alley, R. W. (Robert W.), ill. II. Title.
PZ8.3.P124Bal 1993
[E]—dc20

92-36008
CIP
AC

12 11 6 7 8/9

Printed in the U.S.A. 24

First Scholastic printing, August 1993

THE BALL GAME

by David Packard

Illustrated by R. W. Alley

My First Hello Reader!
With Flash Cards

SCHOLASTIC INC.

New York Toronto London Auckland Sydney

VISITOR 1 0 2 1 0 4
HOME 1 2 0 1 4
2

The game is tied.

I grab my hat.

I'm at the plate.

I swing my bat.

POW

I hit the ball.

I'm running now.

Past first,

past second,

I'm past third.

Wow!

I'm sliding home.

The ball comes in.

I'm safe. I'm safe.

0 2 1 0
4
5
2

We win!

We win!

Act It Out

Action words describe something that is happening. Here are some of the action words in this story:

grab

swing

hit

run

slide

Can you act out these words and tell the story of *The Ball Game* without speaking?

The boy in the story was very happy at the end because his team won. How do you think he would have felt if he lost? Now act out the story showing what would have happened if the other team tagged him out while he was running around the bases.

Long **a**; Short **a**

Some letters make different sounds in different words. The letter **a** is one of those letters. Sometimes the letter **a** has a long **a** sound, as in *game* and *plate*. Other times it has a short **a** sound, as in *hat* and *bat*.

Look at the pictures below. Do these words have long or short **a** sounds?

face

cake

bag

mad

cage

ham

A Funny Story

Sometimes the same word can mean more than one thing. Look at the picture below. What's wrong with these pictures?

The game is tied.

I'm at the plate.

I swing my bat.

I'm sliding home.

1, 2, 3

The boy in the story had to run from first base to second base to third base to home plate, all in the right order. If he had run the bases in the wrong order, his team would not have won the game.

The words in a sentence have to be in the right order for the sentence to make sense. Take your flash cards for these words:

tied

is

game

the

Can you put them in the right order to match the first sentence in the story?

Make other sentences from the story by putting your flash cards in the right order. Can you also make sentences that are not in this story?

A, B, C

Baseball is a game that you play with a bat and a ball. There are games you can play with just words. Here is a word game you and a friend can play.

First think of a word that begins with the letter **a**, such as:

apple

Then have your friend repeat that word and think of a word that begins with the letter **b**, such as:

apple, banana

Then you say the **a** word, the **b** word, and a word that begins with **c**, such as:

apple, banana, carrot

Keep taking turns repeating the words and adding a new word as long as you can until one of you forgets the words that came before.

Answers

(*Long **a**; Short **a***)

Long **a**: face, cake, cage
Short **a**: bag, mad, ham

(*A Funny Story*)

The game is tied means the score of a game is equal for both teams.

I'm at the plate means the player is standing at home plate waiting to bat.

I swing my bat means a player is swinging a baseball bat at a ball.

I'm sliding home means a player is running and sliding in the dirt toward home plate.

(*1, 2, 3*)

The game is tied.